A.J. Cosmo

let's read again.

Soaked © 2015 (2nd ed.)
Thought Bubble Publishing

Written by:
A.J. Cosmo

Illustrated by:
A.J. Cosmo

Editors:
Angela Peason
Mike Kalmbach

Book Layout:
Ricardo-S. Aldape

Production:
Thought Bubble Publishing

A.J. Cosmo

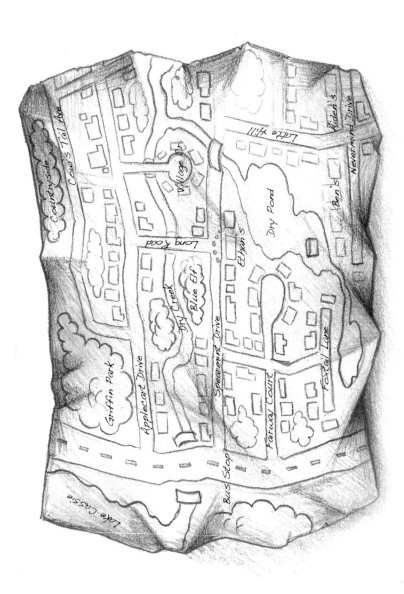

Cowards Run

I'm a coward.

That was the first thing that crossed my mind when the water balloon splattered on Jacob's face. Jacob, the boy who never needed a hall pass. Jacob, the kid who never ate his own lunch. Jacob, the one you cleared the bathroom for.

Cowards don't do this, I thought. *Cowards run.* Let everyone who has ears to hear know that I, Aiden Jones, am a coward.

Jacob let go of Ben's collar and let his victim join my side. Our classmates fell into a sick silence. No one knew what to do because no one had ever challenged Jacob before.

What about me though? What did Jacob have in store for me? Would he drag me into the bathroom and give me a swirly? Would he hold me under the water fountain? Would he stuff my pockets with water balloons and make me do jumping jacks?

Jacob just stared.

The summer sun pulled the water from his shirt, just as it soaked up the moisture from the plants and our skin. Since the drought began in the midwest, our cozy little school had turned into a solar oven. The worst part was that the principal could have cranked up the air conditioning and given us all relief, but she didn't, not even on the last day of school. That's just the kind of lady she was.

"Jacob--I didn't mean to--I mean," I said.

"You almost got my phone wet," he growled.

I gulped. His phone was, of course, the brand new top of the line model that had just come out. His phone was the symbol of his power. He was the top kid at school, so of course he always had the top of the line device. Heard of that new model coming out next month? He already had two. No one knew how he did it. Maybe his dad worked for the cell phone company. Maybe he stole them. Who knew?

The school bell rang, ushering in the second half of the last day of third grade. Kids moved towards the door but Jacob stopped them with a glance. He only had a few moments before the teacher would come to collect us.

"Aiden," Jacob said. His voice felt like sandpaper.

"Jacob," I replied, trying to hide fear in silence.

"See you after school," he said.

I knew what those words meant. Heck, who didn't? After a full year of keeping my head down, I would spend the final hours of school with my neck out.

Jacob walked past me, his shoulder bumping me so hard I fell back. The rest of the class followed behind him with their heads low.

Ben and Ethan, the only two friends I had managed to make in eight months, stayed behind.

"You're dead," Ben said. "I'm dead, too, just a little later," he added as he tried to brush out the hand-print from his collar.

"I'm sure it will wash out," I said.

"Yeah, help me explain that to my parents. Mom will never let me hear the end of it," Ben said. "If your father had his old job we'd be swimming in good shirts!" he mocked.

"It looks fine, Ben," I said, wishing that for once he would comfort me.

"Way to go, Aiden," Ethan said as he hugged me. My back cracked. He didn't mean to hurt me, it's just that Ethan could have taken down Jacob, or any of the teachers for that matter, but he rarely understood what was going on. Ethan is special, which is another way of saying few people want to deal with him.

"I didn't mean to," I said. It still hadn't caught up with me what had just happened. The silence had been broken. Someone had finally stood up to Jacob. I just wished it hadn't been me.

"You did though, so now what?" asked Ben.

"I don't know," I said. "Any ideas?"

"Do you have a will?" Ben jeered.

The second bell rang and our teacher, Mr. Baskwell, waved us inside.

"Why are you boys still out here?" he scolded.

"Sorry Mr. Baskwell," Ben said. "Won't happen again."

"Make sure it doesn't. And what happened to your shirt?" Mr. Baskwell asked.

"Nothing," Ben said as he brushed down his shirt.

I thought about telling Mr. Baskwell the truth, but it was no use, Jacob's power went beyond just kids.

We spent the rest of the last day of class watching the clock wind down. It didn't matter. We were all going to forget whatever they told us in about five hours. There weren't any tests to come back to. No lessons to learn. It's that time of year when you wonder why they go through the bother of teaching us anything in the first place. Without tests, what does it all prove?

Rumors of what had happened on the playground passed with whispers while crumpled up notes offered editorial insights on my fate. It felt like I was the feature story of a cable news network. *'What would happen next? Updates on the hour.'* Within minutes the other kids had ruled on my fate.

"He's probably just going to torture you with the idea that he will do something," Ben whispered. He was trying to be helpful in the worst way possible.

"You think he's that smart?" I replied.

"No talking," said Mr. Baskwell without looking up from his laptop.

Jacob got up and approached the front desk. We all looked up, wondering what he was about to do. A few of the other kids took out their phones and texted the news flash.

"I need to go see my mother," Jacob ordered.

"Can it wait?" Mr. Baskwell asked without any authority.

"No," Jacob said.

"Go quietly then," Mr. Baskwell shrugged.

Jacob glared at me as he went out the door. His eyes felt like a cannon aimed right at my face. The moment he was gone, the room lit up with cell phone screens. Jacob had gone to see his mother. What did it mean? Would the parents get involved? *News as it happens.*

"I need to pee," I blurted out.

Little laughs here and there trickled out.

"We have fifteen minutes till the bell," said Mr. Baskwell, reasserting his authority.

"I really have to go," I said.

More giggling.

"Quiet down," Mr. Baskwell ordered.

I stood up and crossed my legs. I'd probably never live this down, but I had to try something.

"Please, I think I'm going to pee in my pants," I tried one last time.

My classmates burst into laughter.

"You can wait fifteen minutes, Aiden. Now put your head down and wait for the bell," Mr. Baskwell said.

I put my head down on the desk. Seconds passed.

Susan, the hall monitor, quietly walked into the room and handed a note to Mr. Baskwell.

"Aiden," said my teacher.

I looked up, suddenly not wanting to go anywhere. The desk was safe. They couldn't get me here. Susan, not one to delay, handed me the note and motioned for the door.

I had been summoned to the principal's office.

"You can use the bathroom along the way," added Mr. Baskwell.

I didn't move.

"Now!" Mr. Baskwell snapped.

Butt Baths

I paced between the stalls and the sink. I hate the smell of bathrooms. No matter how many urine cakes a place uses, you can't cover up the smell of what's there. What's done is done, stop trying to cover it up and make it smell good.

Maybe I could hide here until the bell rang, I thought.

"Aiden Jones to the principal's office, NOW!" thundered the intercom.

I shook my head. *They couldn't drag me in there with ten bears. I'm not falling into this trap. I'm not walking right into—*

The bathroom door banged open. "Aiden! What are you still doing in here?" Mr. Baskwell asked. "Get going."

I nodded and squeezed through the small opening between him and the door. Then I crept to the main office, dragging my toes along each tile.

Mrs. Shull's door was unusually large for a principal's office. It looked like she special ordered it from some king that had fallen on hard times. The other teachers called it *The Gate*. Gates are never good. They either keep things in or keep things out. Either way that's bad news for whatever is in there.

"Good of you to join us, Aiden," said Mrs. Shull. She was wearing her power suit, blue, with outdated shoulder pads and a sports jacket that was way too warm for the weather. She had a gold hornet brooch on her left breast. She loved hornets and loved to talk about them. How industrious they were. How strong. How protective of their young.

Jacob, her larva, sat across from her.

"Have a seat," she said.

I did. The seat was cold and grabbed me as I sat down. While the rest of the school smoldered, Mrs. Shull's office maintained a refreshingly crisp temperature.

"It seems there was some trouble on the playground," she said.

"I didn't mean to hit him," I lied. I was trying to find a way to politely tell her that her son was evil.

"Then why don't you tell me your side of the story?" she asked.

I looked over at Jacob like the stupid boy I am. "Jacob was filling up water balloons during recess and forcing kids to stuff them in their pants."

"And do what?" Mrs. Shull asked.

"Jumping jacks. He calls them butt baths," I said.

"Why would anyone do that?" she asked.

"Because if you don't have a butt bath you get a stall shower," I explained.

Jacob's fists were clenched and shaking.

"Do I even want to know what that means?" she asked.

"Let's just say that the boys are very grateful to the janitors of this school," I said.

"Jacob," Mrs. Shull said as she turned to her son, "is what Aiden says true?"

"No," Jacob said, totally calm. "He's got it all wrong. I was collecting the balloons from all of the other kids. You see Aiden's been trying to put together a water balloon war all year. The reason he doesn't have any balloons on him was because he gave them all out. He wanted a war."

"Are you even *popular* enough to orchestrate that?" she asked me.

I've never been so happy to be so insulted.

"No," I said. "Jacob had my best friend Ben by the collar and was trying to shove water balloons down his pants. I knew if Ben's cell phone got wet his parents would literally kill him. So I did the only thing I could to stop him."

"How did you get the balloon?" she asked.

"From Timothy Cook, he still had one that hadn't popped in his back pocket."

"He's lying," Jacob shouted.

"Quiet, Jacob," Mrs. Shull growled.

"You started it!" I snapped.

"This little punk almost got my phone wet!" Jacob snarled.

"I SAID QUIET!" Mrs. Shull barked as she stood up.

I'd never seen Jacob afraid before.

Mrs. Shull sat back down in her chair and straightened her hornet brooch.

"I'm very disappointed in you, Aiden," she said. "Your first year here has been wonderfully uneventful. Regardless of your intentions, you should have gotten a teacher."

"They wouldn't have done anything," I whispered.

"Excuse me?" she huffed.

I looked at Jacob, a sneer painted on his face.

No use.

"I'm sorry," I spoke up. "I didn't mean to disappoint you and I didn't mean to put Jacob's phone in danger."

"Go home Aiden," she said. "You're lucky this is the last day of school. I don't want to see you in my office next year, got that?"

"Yes, Mrs. Shull," I said.

"Apologize to Jacob," she added.

I looked at Jacob. I could see the hate in his eyes. I could hear the plans forming in his mind. "I'm sorry I hit you in the face with a water balloon," I said.

The bell rang.

Kids poured into the halls and headed for the door. I went to join them. Jacob's eyes bore into me as I left.

My only two friends in the world were waiting for me by the main entrance.

"How did it go?" Ben asked as I stepped outside the school.

"You okay?" Ethan added.

"Saved by the bell," I said as we got on the bus.

"That it?" asked the bus driver.

"Are you subbing for Mr. Jones?" I asked.

"Nope, I just stole the bus," he replied.

I laughed. "Yeah, that's all of us," I said.

We headed to the back end and threw down our backpacks. The three of us usually sat in the back of the bus where the seats smelled the most, the vinyl had tears, and the bus bounced the highest when it hit potholes. It was the worst place to sit, which is why we usually had it to ourselves.

"So that's it then? Just a talk? What did Jacob say?" Ben asked.

The bus pulled away from the school.

"Saved by the end of the school year," I said as I wiped sweat from my brow. "Next year will be a different story."

"That's good news," Ethan said. "Jacob tried to get you in trouble, but couldn't, so we're free to enjoy the summer."

I could always rely on Ethan to say positive things, even if it made him sound like he didn't know what he was talking about.

"I wish I saw things like you do, Ethan," I said.

As the driver stopped at the first intersection near school, the sound of a hundred cell phones getting a text message echoed through the bus. Ethan and Ben pulled out their phones; mine was silent. I looked around wondering, no, fearing what was happening. That many cell phones going off at once sounds like an explosion.

"Oh boy," Ben said.

"He can't be serious," Ethan chuckled.

"What, what does it say?" I asked.

Ben handed me his phone.

$500 gift card to GameStop and total immunity for the kid that brings me Aiden Jones. –Jacob

I looked up from the phone.

Everyone in the bus stared back at me.

This is Our Stop

"Uh, Aiden," Ben said, drawing out the tail of my name.

"I have eyes," I said.

"What do we do?" Ethan asked in the same tone as a toddler.

Every kid had posted up on their knees and turned around to stare at me. Either they wanted the bounty for themselves, or they wanted to watch someone else collect it. I had only seen the kids like this once before when the local ice cream factory stopped by for free ice cream day. They had us all lined up out front, waiting for that first scoop.

It didn't matter.

"Sit down, everyone," yelled the bus driver. Only half of the kids obeyed.

"What's the plan?" Ben asked. He always asked stuff like that, which was odd, because he always thought he had a better plan.

"We get off at the first stop," I said.

"That's like fifty miles from my house," Ethan said.

"How about you get off and we call for help?" Ben suggested.

"Thanks for sticking your neck out, guys," I said.

The driver turned on his blinker. We were pulling towards the main neighborhood called Mammoth Acres, which was accurate, because the place was unbelievably huge. Some rich New York developer had made the neighborhood twenty years ago. He let his wife name the streets, which was why they all had weird names, and let his cousin, who loved mazes, lay out the streets.

Some say that rich old man headed back to New York and moved on to bigger and better neighborhoods, some say that he went mad because he made the neighborhood too big. And still others say that he's still here, wandering around the neighborhood, never to be seen again.

"We could also just jump out the back door," I said.

"I don't think that thing even works," Ben said as he looked behind us. Funny, it never seems like cars are moving that fast until you look at the road.

The bus brakes screeched and we all lurched forward. The stop sign swung out. The driver looked up in the rear-view mirror. A few kids stood and made their way to the exit.

I started to stand.

Ben pushed me back down. "Not yet."

"Anyone else?" asked the driver with his hand still on the door crank.

The kids were all looking at us, waiting.

The bus driver looked up, seemed to wink, and closed the door. We moved on.

"Wait until no one else gets up," Ben said. "No one is going to come after us if it's too far from home."

I nodded. It sounded reasonable. We just had to hope that no one here liked to walk.

None of the kids had turned around; they just watched us, their heads swaying with the bus. It reminded me of when I went camping with my uncle. In the middle of the night I got out of the tent and shone my flashlight in the field. A hundred eyes reflected back at me. I ran back to the tent as fast as I could.

I don't like camping.

Brakes screeched. Stop sign swung out. The door opened.

No one stood up.

"Anyone?" asked the bus driver.

The bus driver put his hand on the door crank.

"Now," Ben said.

"Wait!" I yelled.

The driver looked up in the mirror.

I stood.

"Guys?" I asked, praying that my friends wouldn't abandon me.

Ethan stood. Ben took a few seconds to join.

We walked single file under the watchful gaze of the driver. The other kids all looked as well, their heads attached to us as we passed by.

So this is what death row feels like.

Someone grabbed me. I pulled back and found another pair of hands on my shoulders. Chaos erupted.

"Stop it!" yelled the bus driver.

I broke free of my backpack and hopped away. The bag landed in the hands of three boys.

"My bag!" I yelled.

"Leave it," Ben said as pushed me forward.

Ethan tried to grab the bag from the kid but the boy punched him.

"He hit me!" Ethan whined.

"Knock it off!" yelled the bus driver as he stood up.

One of the kids grabbed me and pulled me down into the seat. All I could feel were hands holding me down and chatter like rats clamoring in my ears.

"I said knock it off!" yelled the bus driver as he broke apart the crowd and pulled me from the tangle. "What's the matter with you kids?"

No one said a word. They just stared like crows at us.

"Let 'em through, come on, let 'em go," said the bus driver as he pushed the kids away.

"That's not their stop," squeaked a mouse.

The bus driver looked right at me. I had to say something.

"We just bought a new house," I lied.

The bus driver saw the fear in my eyes.

"You boys going to be alright?" he asked.

I nodded.

The bus driver went back to the driver's seat and held back the last of the kids. He stood in the aisle as we stepped out, blocking anyone brave enough to charge out.

We stepped off the bus as the door closed. A moment later it took off and we watched the kids all gather at the back window, their noses pressed against the glass like jackals. They were hungry. How long would that last? What had Jacob done? What had *I* done?

"Well, that was weird," Ben said.

"I thought they were our friends," Ethan said. "John O'Leary hit me. I was always nice to him."

"Thanks for coming with me," I said.

"Not like we had much of a choice," Ben replied. "So what's the plan? Hoof it three miles to Ethan's house?"

"His is the closest. You okay with us coming over, Ethan?" I asked.

"Are you kidding?" Ethan's face lit up. "You're always welcome!" Ethan said.

"Anyone have parents we could call?" Ben asked.

"They don't get home for a while," Ethan said.

"Same here. Dad would be super mad if I called him, too," Ben said.

They looked at me.

I shook my head. My parents, like most of the parents in the neighborhood, both worked jobs to make ends meet. Most of the people in town worked up at the shipping factory named after a jungle at the top of the other hill. And just like that massive jungle, few people ever escaped it.

"Great," Ben said with more sarcasm than a thirteen-year-old girl, "then we're on our own."

"If we cut through the creek, we should be able to make it to the other side of the neighborhood unnoticed. We head to Ethan's and lay low until someone's parents get home," I said. I didn't know where the plan came from; it just sort of rolled out. I was learning that if I didn't think, I did a lot of things that scared me.

"Then what?" Ben asked.

"What do you mean?" I said. I get tired sometimes of Ben asking so many questions. If he wanted to make decisions, he should just say it. I can't stay mad at him though, if you never make a decision, you never have to take the blame for it.

"We just wait there until summer is over? What about when school starts?" Ben asked. "What do we do when Jacob is back there waiting for us? Have you ever had a butt bath in winter? We don't even know what he's told his mom, either. What if he gets us into summer school over this?"

"How could he get us in there?" Ethan asked, scared.

"He's Jacob Shull, he gets to do whatever he wants," Ben said.

"Stop it, you're scaring him," I said.

"He is not," Ethan whimpered. "What are we going to do though, Aiden?"

"I don't know, man," I said.

Ben shook his head and sweat flew off. He wiped his forehead. "It's like two hundred degrees out here today."

"At least if Jacob soaks us," Ethan said, "it will feel good."

"Speak for yourself," Ben said, "If this phone gets wet, I'm dead and I'm not just saying that either. I think my folks would be happy with the savings."

"Don't say that," Ethan said. "They love you."

Ben shrugged.

"Let's go," I said.

We walked up the street toward a pair of remarkably similar houses that had a path cut between them. The path would lead to a dry creek and hopefully on to Ethan's house. When we were younger we used to call the houses the guardian twins. They were the gateway to the creek, a land of mystery where countless people venture. We used to imagine that we were explorers in an undiscovered world filled with trolls and wood faeries. Who knew what lay beyond the twins? Fame? Fortune? Death?

Legend has it that a pair of Canadian twins once owned the houses. Everything they did had to be exactly the same. They got married at the same time. Moved to the same town. Got the same job at a factory. Built the same house. Decorated it the same way. And did everything in their power to keep their lives the same. Except when one of their wives became pregnant, the other pair found out that they couldn't conceive.

The brothers never spoke again.

When we neared the space between the houses, we heard a front door open and a screen door slam shut. A pudgy kid with a tuft of hair covering his eyes and a drop of snot dangling from his nose stepped out.

Every gate has its keeper.

In his arms rested a massive Super Soaker.

He pumped it and took aim at me.

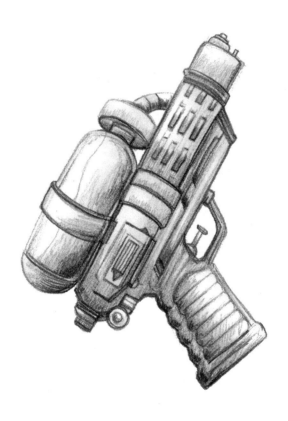

Safe Passage

"Heya Aiden." The kid sniffled and wiped his nose on his arm.

"Hey Sam. How you feeling?" I said. Sam Wadden always had allergies. The school nurse was convinced that the kid was allergic to himself. All that sniffling and sneezing made it easy for his parents to let him stay inside and play video games all day. Sam also loved sweets and his body showed it.

"Pretty good, pretty good. You mind, um, coming inside?" Sam motioned toward his door with the water gun.

"Weren't you home sick from school today?" I asked.

"You can't catch it, trust me," he said. His hands trembled. "I've got this new game I want to show you."

"Still, Sam, I can't afford to get sick. Not worth the risk," I said as I pushed Ben and Ethan toward the alley.

"You sure?" Sam asked as he stepped toward us.

"We're sure," Ben said. "You got something dripping from your chin," pointing out the brain tickler that dangled from Sam's nose.

"Maybe we could come back and try out that game soon though," Ethan added. "You know, after you feel better."

Sam fired. Water splattered on Ben's knee. He shrieked. "My phone!"

We ran between the houses and into the forest. Sam gave chase, yelling until he went into a coughing fit. He stopped to catch his breath, cursing us as he sneezed.

"Poor guy," Ethan said.

"That was close," I said. "Not all of the other kids are gonna be sick like that."

Ben frantically pulled out his cell phone and checked. A few droplets flecked the screen. He wiped it off and cradled it to his chest.

"Is it okay?" I asked.

He clicked the unlock screen and a picture lit up. He stared up at me like I had kicked his puppy. "Too close," he said. "I'm not gonna lie, Aiden, I don't like this one bit."

"We're gonna be fine. No one is gonna get wet," I said.

"What do we do, chief?" Ethan asked.

We heard a commotion from Sam's house and ducked behind some trees. Some other kids from down the street had heard we stopped near the gates and had run to find us. They joined Sam and followed him toward us.

"Everyone wants that gift card," I said, "That means an army will be waiting for us at my house."

"Or Ethan's or mine," Ben said.

"Right," I said. "So if this is war, then we need weapons."

"I don't want to fight anybody," Ethan said. "Can't we just talk to them?"

"We have to defend ourselves," I said as I put my hand on Ethan's shoulder. "I know this sucks, I'm sorry."

"There they are!" Sam yelled and then sneezed.

Sam led the charge toward us.

"Run!" I yelled and we ran deeper into the woods.

The trees gave way to a dry creek that snaked through the back of the neighborhood. It had been flowing once, all three inches of it, but the hot summer had worn the water down and now all that was left was cracked dirt and parched grass. The creek was a highway, a long and winding straight shot to safety. The only problem was the complete lack of hiding places.

Ben frowned at our footprints. "Maybe leaving a trail isn't such a good idea."

"Stick to the sides then and head back into the trees," I said.

We pushed through the forest and towards the houses at the north end of the neighborhood. Their fences formed a long wall that kept us caged between it and the exposed creek bed. At any moment Sam and his minions would catch up to us. We had to find a way through the fence, somewhere safe.

"There," I said as I pointed to a log playhouse that peeked above the white fence.

"A playhouse? Isn't that a little obvious?" Ben sneered.

"Ethan, can you help me up?" I asked, ignoring Ben.

Ethan made a step with his hands and vaulted me up over the fence. I struggled and fell over. Ben followed behind, falling to the ground beside me.

"You okay?" I asked.

"Just perfect," Ben said as he dusted himself off. He checked his phone and then helped me pull Ethan into the backyard.

"Quiet," I whispered. Through the fence we heard Sam's gang kick up a storm. They ran up to the fence and hit it with the butt of their water guns. Boards shook as they thundered past, pounding and shouting.

"We're gonna find you, *aaachooo*, Aiden!" Sam sniffled and spit on the ground.

"Gross man, get a tissue," one of the other kids said.

The noise died down as the planks trembled to the next fence.

We took a moment to catch our hearts.

"Where are we?" Ethan asked as he stepped away from the fence. We had fallen into a pristine backyard of a family with a good amount of money. All of the landscaping had been manicured by hired hands and the whole place looked like a spread from Better Homes and Gardens.

"Jimmy Valoran's house," I said.

Ben shook his head. "Jimmy's bad news, man.

Why on earth would you drag us here?"

"He can help," I said as I walked towards the little log playhouse that was nestled in the side of the yard.

I went to knock on the door but Jimmy had already opened it.

He stared out from behind his glasses and grinned, showing off his braces.

"I've been expecting you."

We sat around a pink table on princess chairs.

Negotiations

My head barely cleared the ceiling and Ethan's didn't at all. He instead sat hunched over in his chair, unable to look up from the ground.

Jimmy was short enough to sit comfortably. He had elegance about him, poise, as if he could do anything at any moment and no one would question it. He had decorated the cabin like an office, even going so far as to put a small plastic plant in the corner and to hang framed, important looking, documents on the wall.

There was also some oddly out of place girl stuff: pink blankets, unicorns, hair clips, not to mention the whole table set.

"My dad's been making me share with my sister," Jimmy said, knowing exactly what was going through everyone's mind.

"I like it," Ethan said as his poor seat crumpled beneath him.

"Can I offer you a juice pouch?" Jimmy asked.

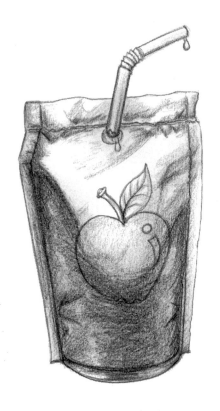

"No, thank you," I said even though I was parched. You see, that's the thing with Jimmy Valoran, everything comes with a price, even things that he offers seemingly free. A concept that I don't think Ben ever grasped.

"Hi Jimmy," Ben said, an obvious hint of disdain in his tone.

"Hello yourself, Benny. How's math going?" Jimmy asked. Jimmy smiled the kind of smile you make when you pull wings off a fly.

Ben gritted his teeth.

"We need your help," I said, not wanting to watch Ben any longer.

Jimmy smelled his straw and took a sip from his fruit drink.

"And here I thought you just wanted to hang out," he said.

"Water guns. You got them or not?" I asked. I knew how Jimmy worked. You had to cut through his appearance and stop all of the little rituals. The longer things took, the worse the deal you'd get.

"That depends on what you have to offer," Jimmy replied.

I emptied my pockets. "Ten dollars and an iTunes gift card with seven bucks left on it."

Ethan did the same. "Six dollars and my Charmander keychain." Ethan laid the stuff on the table.

"My favorite Pokémon." Jimmy took another sip of juice. He looked at Ben. "Anything else?"

"Please," I said to Ben. "We need whatever we can get."

Ben huffed and pulled out his wallet. "I have five bucks."

"Looks like there's a little more than that," Jimmy said.

"Ben," I asked once more.

"I'm not giving him everything!" Ben said as he threw the five-dollar bill and put his wallet back. "It's bad enough you're even dragging me here in the first place."

"That's all we got," I said. "Now can you help us or not?"

Jimmy took the offerings. He counted the money, pocketed it, and then, put the Charmander on his house keys.

"That gets you this." Jimmy swiveled around and opened a cabinet full of water guns. My jaw dropped. Jimmy's arsenal had every model of every brand of water gun on the market. He had guns that had been discontinued, guns that had been recalled, he even had the legendary gun that parents had protested against, the one that was so powerful that the manufacturer now sells it as riot gear.

The magnificent Eaudezeus. Hand crafted by the finest toy makers in China. Somehow Jimmy had gotten the special gold edition. It shimmered with a soft light, almost too cool to exist.

"Is that?" I squeaked.

Jimmy smiled. "Oh this?" he said as he picked up the Eaudezeus. "Just a little thing I found at a flea market. It took three years of searching to get one. You know eBay won't even allow these to be sold? Something about being dangerous."

"Do your parents know you have one?" Ben asked.

"My parents know whatever they know, the rest is none of their business," Jimmy said as he put the gun back. "Unfortunately, you don't have nearly enough to merit such a fine piece of equipment. I'm afraid that Charmander can fetch only this."

He reached in and grabbed three small water pistols.

"That's it?" Ben said.

Jimmy frowned. "Unless you have something more to offer."

Jimmy and Ben stared at each other until I broke through.

"It will do," I said as I took one of the water guns. Ethan grinned as he claimed one as well.

Jimmy sipped his juice and watched Ben. The packet ran out of liquid and wrinkled into the straw. Jimmy kept sucking until the dry pouch sound scratched our ears.

"Something wrong?" Jimmy asked.

Ben shook his head. "I don't like this."

"Ben, it's a done deal. Just take it," I said.

"He gave me bad answers," Ben said. "This kid does bad deals, that's how he makes his money."

"I'm not responsible for teachers changing tests at the last minute," Jimmy said. "And if you call responsible capitalism bad, then you are going to have a very difficult life."

"You paid for answers?" I asked looking over at Ben, probably like his mother would have.

"We're not all brilliant like you, Aiden." Ben grudgingly took the water gun and slipped it under his waistband.

"To business," Jimmy said as he toasted the empty juice packet.

We had nothing to drink, so we just stared at him.

"Now, gentlemen, if you don't mind, I have important matters to attend to," Jimmy said as he motioned towards the door.

We got up and crawled out of the log cabin, only to come face to hose with Jimmy's little sister, Veronica. She had her thumb over the end of a hose and the rest of the line wrapped to the side of her little pink dress.

"About five hundred dollars' worth of business, to be exact," Jimmy said.

Veronica crimped the hose in one hand and pointed the nozzle at my face.

She smiled.

To Be Expected

"Easy now," I said as I raised my hands. "Your name's Veronica, right? Courtney babysat you. She used to babysit me too."

"Quit yapping, cootie walrus," Veronica hefted the hose. We backed up against the playhouse.

"I don't have cooties," Ethan said.

"You're a thick *Odobenus*, aren't you?" Veronica snapped.

Ethan put up his hands.

Jimmy came out with his golden gun.

"Good work, sis," Jimmy said with a smile.

"Just keep your end of the bargain," she said.

"Three tea parties," Jimmy said. "I'm not going to kiss any dolls though."

"It's five tea parties. Stop trying to change the deal," Veronica turned her hose on her brother for the briefest of moments.

Veronica was only six, but in between dance recitals and cupcake parties she had grown a cutthroat reputation, even among the kids in my grade. She was the prettiest of vipers.

"I want to come to the tea party," Ethan said honestly.

"Let us go, Jimmy, and Ethan will have the tea parties in your place," I said.

"No cootie walruses allowed!" Veronica shrieked as she stomped her foot. "You're going to get cooties everywhere!"

"Doesn't seem like Veronica likes Ethan, friend, so no deal," Jimmy said. "Now if you don't mind, I have a text to send."

Jimmy pulled out his cell phone and made it a little too clear he was texting Jacob.

I caught Ben's eye, and nodded to Ethan, making sure that they caught the signal.

Veronica raised the hose. "Don't try anything."

I lowered my hand toward my pocket. "I just have a message I have to check."

"I'm warning you!" Veronica barked.

I jerked my hands back up.

Jimmy finished the text and hit send. He went to put away his phone.

"Now!" I yelled.

Veronica un-crimped the hose. A rocket of water shot out, but I dove to the side and tackled Ben. The water sprayed past us, soaking Jimmy from head to toe.

He dropped his drenched cell phone. It bounced on the concrete, and the screen cracked.

I scrambled to my feet and pulled Ben up.

"Veronica!" Jimmy screamed. "Look what you did!"

The hose hung limp in her hands. "I didn't mean to!"

"They're getting away!" Jimmy screamed.

Veronica turned and unleashed the hose, but we were already at the gate. Ethan threw open the door and I slammed it back just as a spray of water exploded against it.

We headed to the street and up the hill.

Jimmy's frustrated yells echoed through the neighborhood.

We ran until our feet swelled in our shoes. The sun beat down overhead. Even in the late afternoon it must have been well over a hundred degrees out.

"Just soak me," Ben said. "I can't take this heat. I mean, it wouldn't be that bad, right?"

"We're almost there," I said, "Just a few more blocks."

"You think you could claim that gift card yourself?" Ben asked.

"Are you wanting to turn me in?" I asked, half sarcastic.

Ben's phone suddenly dinged.

"Another message?" I asked.

Ben read the text and his face fell.

"What's wrong?" Ethan asked.

"Jacob's offering prizes for me and you too, Ethan," Ben said.

"What? Why?" Ethan asked, confused.

"You're helping me," I said softly. "I'm sorry guys."

"That's the start of an apology," Ben said.

"What do you want me to say? Jacob would be after you no matter what. After all, you dodged him today."

"Yes, and thank you for that, but this is getting way out of hand," Ben said.

"Guys, look," Ethan interrupted. He pointed down the street towards his yellow house. A group of boys had set up a patrol around the perimeter.

"You've got to be kidding me," I said.

"They have bikes," Ben noted. "You think they recruited the Motocrossers?"

"I hope not. Come on, this way. Maybe we can flank them," I said.

"What's *flank* mean?" Ethan asked.

"It means to go to the side of," I said. "It's a military term."

"We're at war, kiddo," Ben said.

"Oh," Ethan said. "Isn't that bad?"

We walked the property lines on the south side of the street. Eventually, we came back to the dry creek and crossed it, arriving on the north side of the Candy Ridge cul-de-sac. That's when we saw the first of Jacob's surprises.

They sat on their bikes in a group of seven- a ragtag bunch of bullies and rough kids that must have ditched school early and still gotten the text. Each one of them was sweating from top to bottom, a problem that could have been solved with one of their many large water guns.

"That's a heck of a welcoming committee," Ben said.

"How did they know where my house was?" Ethan asked.

"It's pretty common knowledge," Ben said. "Everyone knew after your parents invited the whole school to your birthday party."

"But nobody came to my party!" Ethan said.

Ben put his hand on Ethan's shoulder. "Exactly, buddy, exactly."

"We came to your party," I said.

"Yeah, thanks," Ethan said, confused. He had a blank look on his face like the whole world was a lie.

"Anyway, it doesn't look like those guys are here for a party. Any ideas, commander?" Ben sneered.

"We make a run for it. Just cut through their lines and make it to the front door," I said. "Once inside, we hold out there until our parents get home."

"That could be hours," Ethan said, still reeling.

"Do you leave your front door unlocked?" Ben asked Ethan.

"Oh, uh, yeah. There's a spare key under a fake

rock. The lock's old though, sometimes it gets stuck," Ethan replied.

"Sounds like a solid plan," Ben said.

"You have any better ideas?" I asked.

"A few," Ben said with a smirk.

"Look," I said. "If we can just get inside, this will all be over. I think it's worth a shot."

"You really think this will just pass over? You started a storm, Aiden, and we don't have a basement," Ben said.

I rolled my eyes. "Are you done?" I asked.

"Aye, aye, captain," Ben said.

"Alright then, let's do this," I said. "You two take the sides. I'll make a distraction. At least that way if anything goes bad I'll be the only one soaked."

We split up. Ben and Ethan took opposite sides of the streets and followed close to the front doors. I took the middle of the street, heading straight for the blockade.

"Hey guys!" I raised my hands and waved. "Over here, I heard you were looking for me!"

"It's him!" one of the guards yelled. The other boys scrambled into position, raising their water guns over their bikes.

I approached.

"I'm surrendering peacefully," I yelled. "There's no need for any of that."

Ethan and Ben slipped past them as I spoke. We only needed a few minutes.

"Hold it right there!" a boy named Tim Randal called out.

I froze.

Tim was second in the bully pecking order at the school. He and Jacob had an uneasy pact at school. In short, Tim got Jacob's leftovers. While Jacob dominated the playground and terrorized the bathrooms, Tim had control over the cafeteria and milk breaks. He was best known for giving kids white snot.

White snot is where you force someone to drink milk and then tickle or punch them in the stomach causing milk to spurt out of their nose. It burns, especially if it's chocolate, and your snot will be mixed with milk for the rest of the day.

"You armed?" Tim asked.

I nodded and pulled the water gun from my pocket. Lot of help Jimmy turned out to be.

"Put it down on the ground in front of you," he said.

I put the water gun on the asphalt. Ethan reached the door and pulled out his keys. Ben looked up from the bushes.

"Kick it to me," Tim said.

I did, but the gun didn't go far; I'm not the best at sports.

Ethan struggled with the door. Of course, it had jammed. Of course, it took time. Luckily, none of the other boys had noticed yet.

"So, which one of you gets the gift card?" I yelled out.

The kids exchanged glances.

"We're splitting it," Tim yelled. "Ain't that right?"

The other boys nodded like they had all discussed it before, though they clearly hadn't.

"Oh yeah? Who gets what?" I yelled.

Seven mercenaries. Five hundred dollars. That leaves about seventy bucks apiece.

"I'm getting the new Xbox," one of the other kids said.

"You won't get enough for that, dummy," someone else said.

"Wait, how much are we each getting?" Another kid counted on his fingers.

"It's not very much," I said. "I don't even know if you have enough for a game after tax and everything. Maybe you could afford a used game, but who would want that?"

"Stop it. We split it even. He's trying to distract us!" Tim yelled.

"I don't even think they'll let you split the gift card. You guys will all just have to share whatever you buy," I added, knowing that if bullies hate anything, it's giving stuff to other bullies.

Just then, one of the soldiers turned around and saw Ethan and Ben at the front door.

"Look!" he yelled. "His friends!"

Tim turned around. The patrol rushed the front door. I ran straight into the crowd after my friends.

Water streams shot out from all sides.

I ducked through the barrage just as Ben and Ethan ran towards me. The whole mess of kids collided.

Ben frantically fired as Ethan ducked down. Three of the other kids grabbed me and pulled me away.

"Aiden!" Ethan yelled. He grabbed my arm and wrestled me free. He pushed me out of the ring of boys and I joined Ben as he ran up the hill. Streams of water licked our feet. I looked over at Ben as he ran by my side. He looked terrified. Forget cell phones, those kids were out for blood. I couldn't blame him though; I was scared, too. The thought crossed my mind that I should just surrender, give up, and spare my friends whatever was going to happen.

I couldn't do that though. Like I said, *I'm a coward.*

We were a block from the house before we realized Ethan wasn't with us and there was no time to go back.

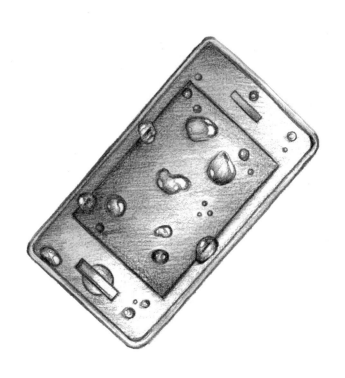

Casualties of War

Slightly to the northwest of Ethan's house sits one of five large forest areas in Mammoth Acres. They're called parks by the Home Owners Association, but it's a poorly kept secret that they're just undeveloped plots that no one wants to pay to trim. The park we ran into is called Blue Elf Grove. Again, they sort of ran out of good names when they made our neighborhood.

We ran into the woods and weaved through the trees. Ben grabbed my hand and pulled me into one of the crusty drainpipes that marked where future homes would be put. We waited there for the patrol to run past.

"You left him," Ben said.

"You left him? How about we left him?" I said.

"It was your idea to make a break for it. Your plan, your blame," Ben growled.

We stopped, looked out of the pipe, and waited for the sound of the rallying kids to come near.

"I'm sorry," I said as I looked down at the dirt.

Feet stomped by overhead and we dropped our voices.

Ben shook his head. "They're not after me," Ben whispered. "I could walk out right now and no one would care."

"Don't say that," I said. I couldn't help but feel a bit betrayed. "What makes you think they wouldn't bother you?"

"I nearly got soaked back there." He pulled out his cell phone. He looked at his phone as if it was the most precious thing in the world. And you know what? To him, it was. I knew that if something happened to it that it would take at least three grades before he would be able to get a new one.

"Is it okay?" I asked, not caring about the phone at all.

He tapped the phone. Then he shook it, pawed it, *and pleaded with it.*

It didn't work.

"Let me see," I said.

Ben threw the phone at me. It fell down, but I caught it just before it hit the concrete.

I flicked the power button and then held it to force a reset. When that didn't help, I pulled off the back of the phone and reset the battery. A bit of water dripped out.

Nothing.

The phone was dead, as dead as I was.

"I'm sorry," I said.

Ben didn't hear me, or he didn't acknowledge me. He just took the phone back and let it hang in his hands.

"I'll help you get a new one," I said. "I can get a summer job. Who knows, if I get a job at the shipping plant I could afford a brand new one for you."

Ben said nothing. He couldn't look at me, or he didn't want to look at me. He just stewed there, not thinking of anything clever to say.

I hate it when people do that. They want you to say something, but nothing you could say would be right, so they just sit in silence and wait for you to make the next move. It's always a trap.

"I'm kind of running out of ways to apologize here," I finally said.

"Then stop apologizing. You can end this," he said. "Walk up there and give yourself up. Let Jacob have his way with you. Maybe you'll get lucky and he will make it quick."

"I can't end it like that," I said, not really understanding what I meant. I felt that I couldn't let Jacob get away with harassing me, or anyone else for that matter. Something had to be done about the kid, but I didn't know what that something was.

"Why not? What's stopping you? Why did you even run in the first place?"

I stared at Ben. I didn't understand why I stood up to Jacob, but I knew I did it for him. I wanted to hit Ben. I wanted to tell him off. I wanted to go back in time and let Jacob give him that butt bath.

You know what though, deep inside of me I knew that I *didn't* do it for Ben. I did it for a totally different reason. A reason I just had to act on.

That didn't make sense though, after all, *I'm a coward.*

"Friends stick by their friends," I said. "Even when things get rough."

"Really? Like how you stuck by Ethan?" Ben asked.

"I thought he was with us," I said. "It was too late to go back."

"You shed him so that you could get away. You let that idiot take the fall for you because you're too chicken to stand up to Jacob yourself."

"And you aren't?" I said. "Where was that fight when Jacob had you by the collar? And don't you dare call Ethan an idiot. He's our friend. Or did you forget that?"

"Did you?" Ben said.

The argument collapsed into silence.

"Come on. He's gonna be fine," I said quietly. "There's nothing they want from him."

Ben sat silent for still longer.

"I'm done," he said.

"Done with what?" I asked.

"I said I'm done," Ben said as he left the drainpipe. I crawled out and watched him go.

"Ben," I pleaded. "Please don't."

Ben walked out of the forest and went home. I didn't see where he went or if any of the bullies had caught up to him. To me, he just vanished in the forest, leaving me to rot in the drainpipe.

Ben was right about one thing, though, there was a storm coming, and I didn't have any shelter.

I didn't have a choice.

The only place I had access to, my home, was all the way at the other end of the neighborhood. To get there I would have to cross paths with every kid that got that text message. I could take the long way and wrap around the east side of the neighborhood or, stupidly, I could wade through the dry lake and be so exposed that anyone within a half-mile would see me. Neither option seemed like a good idea.

No matter what though, when I got home, Jacob would be waiting for me.

The Calvary

I was frustrated. No, I was angry. I just wanted to curl up in a little ball in that drainpipe and wait for the September rain. Maybe I could at least hide here until my parents got worried, sent out a search team, and celebrated when they found me here. I could tell the police that I was hiding from a bunch of thugs, criminals even, or better yet that I had escaped a slave trade. I would be a hero. I would be so loved that Jacob couldn't touch me.

Or maybe my parents wouldn't believe me. Maybe they would call me a troublemaker. Maybe my parents wouldn't even bother to look. That's not a far stretch, seeing as how they barely notice I'm there as it is.

I should have let Ben take a butt bath. Who knows? Maybe Ben deserved it. How could I know what kind of kid Ben really was? I mean, yeah, I had been his friend for six months now, but how much can you really learn about a person in that time? Heck, I've known myself for nine years and I still don't know

the first thing about myself. Maybe I should have been right up there with Jacob, helped him even, show Ben a thing or two.

No. Stop that.

Poor Ethan. I did just leave him behind. Who knows what those kids are doing to him, or what Jacob will do to him? Did Ethan even understand what was going on? Did he think it was all a game? Did he feel betrayed too, just like Ben, and if so, would he have agreed with Ben or gotten mad at him? Sometimes, I think Ethan is smarter than all of us, and we're all just the dumb kids who care about the wrong things.

Shadows crept across the creek as the sun moved overhead. Four-thirty, I guessed by the look of it. Just a little while longer and our parents would be home. I could stop running. I could stop fighting. I could just crash in my room and pull the covers over my head, imagine a better summer, a better school, and better friends.

I'd be safe.

I could stay home all summer. Or maybe convince my parents to send me to a camp that I am far too old for, one where *I* could be the one in charge and call the shots. No one would mess with me because I was three years older than the next oldest. Heck, I could be a counselor. Tell all the kids that some crazy monster was hiding under their beds. Scare them real good. You're safe when people are afraid of you.

Stop that.

My parents would never send me to camp again, not after the fit I threw last time. No, I'd be stuck at home all summer. In a prison I created myself.

I had to do something.

What though?

I crawled out of the pipe and looked around.

Sunlight beamed down with such force that you could hear it baking the grass. We called it a forest, but if the rains didn't come soon, it wouldn't even make good firewood. If you listened closely, you could hear the wood asking for water. It sounded like a buzz, a hornet sound, whirling through the air.

I wiped sweat from my brow as I headed through the woods.

The buzzing grew louder. Trees groaned. I realized it wasn't a natural sound.

"Dirt bikes!" I yelled.

Stupid, stupid boy. You traded regular bike kids for the Motocrossers. Those kids were from the countryside. They hung out together, biked together, and generally did things much rougher than anyone from the neighborhood. They had to; the countryside is a rough place.

The first motorcycle came from the right and darted through the trees ahead of me. Dust and dirt splattered in its wake. I covered my eyes and spit out the debris.

A blue helmet turned back and my stomach fell. The kid revved the bike and swung back my way. I ran like a rabbit.

I ducked between trees, swerving in and out, as the bike carved a path parallel to me. He cut me off, but I turned around and ran in the other direction.

Buzzing came from all around. It sounded like a swarm of hornets protecting their nest.

I ducked under a fallen tree as three more bikes joined the first: red, green, blue, orange, just as I feared. They're farmers, they lived and worked in cornfields. I couldn't stay hidden for long.

How many people did Jacob text?

Orange and Green crossed in front of me, stopping me cold. Blue and Red came up from behind, their arms held out, their hands held together.

I ducked.

Red and Blue missed me and accidental-ly clothes-lined Orange. The kid fell to the ground and rolled with the force of his bike. The other kids stopped and looked back, making sure he was all right. They glared at me. Even threw the helmets I saw that they were mad.

I darted to the south of the forest and headed for the houses.

"He's headed out!" yelled Green.

I made it out of the forest and stumbled onto Spearmint Drive. A blue sedan appeared. I froze. The car swerved and barely avoided me. I turned around and waved at it, screaming at the top of my lungs, beg-ging the drivers to stop.

He did.

I didn't expect that.

The car backed up, idled, and an old man rolled down the window. He stared at me with distrust, won-dering why I had almost made him hit me.

"You okay, son?" he said, less concerned for my well-being than I'd have liked.

"Can you give me a ride?" I begged.

Orange pulled up behind me and cut off his bike. He pulled off his helmet and smiled at the older man.

"Oh hey, Mr. Hanson. How are you doing?" said Orange.

The man's face lit up when he recognized the kid.

"Kenny, what are you boys up to?" asked the man.

"Oh, nothing, just racing in the creek," said Orange.

"They were chasing me," I said. "All of them, they're trying to capture me."

"Yeah, that's kind of the point of the game, you know," said Orange. "Except someone's trying to cheat." He elbowed my chest like we were old chums.

Mr. Hanson glanced between us.

"Please," I mouthed.

I saw that Mr. Hanson understood. He knew that I was in trouble. He knew that he could help me. He knew that he could easily offer me a ride and everything would be okay. However, like adults oftentimes do, Mr. Hanson found it much easier to do nothing at all. When you get involved helping someone else you obligate yourself to their needs, and no one needs *more* obligations.

"Tell your mom hello for me, Kenny. Oh, and

let her know that the church luncheon has been moved from the tenth to the seventeenth. Could you do that for me?" said Mr. Hanson.

"Got it, Mr. Hanson," said Orange with a Cheshire smile. "I'll see you at church."

Church, I thought to myself, how appropriate.

"You boys have fun, and no cheating," he smiled at me.

"Yeah, no cheating," I said solemnly.

The blue sedan took off and an X-Games bumper sticker caught my eye. Of course Mr. Hanson was into motocross; nothing was going to give me a break. Orange smiled at me.

Hornets buzzed and then died as Red, Green, and Blue pulled up next to me.

"Well now, Aiden," said Orange. "That was a close one."

Lords of War

"You going to call Jacob now?" I asked.

"In time," Orange said.

The others leaned forward on their handlebars.

"I'm over this, just take me to Jacob. He can't do anything worse," I said. And I was over it. Mr. Hanson's apathy proved how hopeless the whole situation had become.

"That's the plan, kiddo, but we need to do business first," Orange said with a hiss that would have made Jimmy proud.

"Business?" I asked. Though I knew exactly what he meant.

"Oh yeah. You don't think we're just going to hand you over? The way we see it, if he's this desperate to get you, then there's no reason why he wouldn't give a little more."

The other colors nodded along, like they had been planning this for weeks. I guess you fight for every angle out in the cornfields.

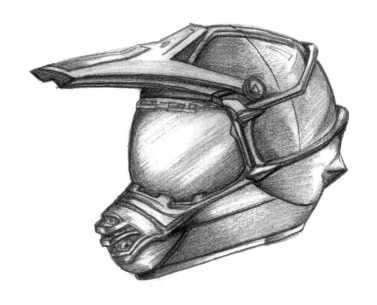

"Don't go down that road," I said. "You don't want to end up on his list as well."

"We ain't scared of Jacob," Blue said. "We ain't scared of no one."

"Except maybe an English teacher," I said.

"We're two grades over him," Orange said. "Next year we're in high school and his mom can't touch us."

"And you don't think she's friends with the High school principal?" I asked, just guessing. "You don't know what Jacob is capable of."

"That's enough out of you," Orange said.

"Car!" yelled Green.

Orange pulled me to the sidewalk and the other boys walked their motorcycles back. A blue SUV came into view and slowed down as it neared us. I didn't bother waving for help, what's the use; I just hoped that the sight of someone strangling my shoulder would be enough of a sign.

The SUV slowed down and the window cracked. A middle-aged woman with bags under her eyes looked out of the car. She saw Orange's grip on my shoulder, saw the way that my shirt bunched under his hand, and saw the tired, painful, look in my eyes.

And she didn't care.

A braver kid would have broken free and gotten in her car, whether she liked it or not. Then again, I'm not brave: *I'm a coward.*

"You kids should stay off the road," she sighed.

"Will do, ma'am," Orange said.

She rolled up her window and drove off, never hearing the handful of awful names the color gang called her under their breath.

"Not your lucky day, Aiden," Orange said as he pulled out his cellphone and sent a text.

We waited.

"How much are you asking for?" I asked.

Red smiled. "A grand."

"Seriously?" I asked, stunned.

"Enough for a PlayStation and an Xbox," Green said.

"And a few games," Blue added.

"For each of you? That's not enough money," I said.

"We can share," snapped Red.

"We ain't spoiled like you neighborhood kids," said Green.

Orange's cellphone dinged.

We waited for him to read it.

Orange's face fell.

"What?" Blue asked.

"Seth? It's your report card," Orange said, puzzled. He handed the phone to Red.

"Let me see that," Red read the text and shook his head. "That's not cool, man. That's not cool!"

"He didn't go for the deal, did he?" I said.

"That's bull crap! I got an A in science!" Red yelled.

"Give me that." Blue grabbed the phone. "It says you got a D."

"Yeah, and the same for Gym. Gym!" Red screamed. "I could ace that in my sleep!"

The phone buzzed again.

"Um, Trevor," Red handed the phone to Blue.

"He's changing our grades! Kenny, he's changing our grades!" Blue yelled.

"Calm down," Orange said.

"Calm down? Calm down! What do you think Dad's gonna do to me!" Blue screamed as he clenched his helmet. "I'm going to be shucking for weeks!"

"Cut the offer, tell him we'll take three hundred," Green said.

I shook my head. "It's not going to work," I whispered.

Orange took back the phone and texted.

We waited.

The phone buzzed.

"No deal," Orange said. "He pulled everything off the table, says that we're all in summer school unless we turn him over right now."

"He can't do that," Red said. "We're going to Six Flags. He can't do that!"

"He can do whatever he wants," I said. "You should have known better."

"I say we drag Aiden to him, turn him over before it's too late," Green said.

"The kid's toxic, he's gonna bring the whole school down. Let's tie him to a tree for the wolves," Blue said.

Orange texted Jacob again.

"Let him go. Teach Jacob a lesson for messing with my grades," Red said.

"I'm with him," I said.

Orange's cell-phone beeped.

"Quiet," Orange ordered.

Something had changed. We all leaned in to learn what.

"Jacob told us to meet him at 102 Nevermind Drive, he'll give us the gift card then."

"That's my address," I said.

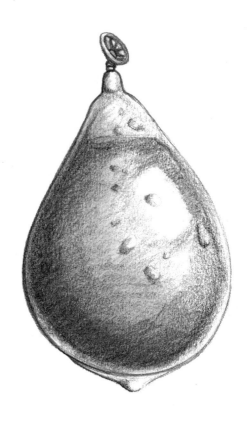

Homecoming

Our shadows cast across the neighborhood as we crossed Latte Hill. My hands were bound with bungee chords that gave me rug burns as I walked. Orange had another chord wrapped around my waist and he pulled me along with his bike. I'd stumble every few feet only to get yanked forward.

He cut the engine and kicked the stand.

Jacob had arranged two defensive lines of well-armed kids at the front of my house in an arrow formation. They had water pistols, Super Soakers, tubs of water balloons, and even a pair of Koziltek M-44 water bazookas--the kind that the homeowners association had banned from the neighborhood three years ago.

Jacob stood in the center of the formation, his shoulders held back like a Marine. He wore a white tank top and some swim trunks and had two water pistols strapped to his belt and a Super Soaker sniper rifle slung over his back.

"Bring him here," Jacob yelled.

Orange shoved me down the hill.

The kids surrounding Jacob all pointed their water guns at me. I don't know why. My hands were bound and I wouldn't have done anything even if they were free.

"Look at what the cat dragged in," sneered Jacob.

"I think he just called you a cat," I said to Orange.

"What did you say, tough guy?" Jacob said.

I lowered my head.

"Yeah, that's what I thought," Jacob said.

Orange cleared his throat.

"A deal's a deal," Orange said.

"I'll get it to you in a few days, cool?" Jacob asked.

"Not cool," Orange said. His brothers raised their water guns.

Jacob's army raised theirs.

Water sloshed about.

"Easy now," Jacob said. "Everyone stand down."

I wanted to say something, something snide, witty, something that would make the other kids laugh, something that would embarrass Jacob. Make him pay just a little before he got his revenge on me. I didn't want to say something clever after this was all over, like how the best lines usually come. I wanted to do something *now*.

Think. Come on. Think.

"Who gets the gift card, Jacob?" I asked loudly.

"Shut your mouth," Jacob snapped.

"The delivery guys," Orange said. His brothers nodded.

"What about us?" asked Michael McClain, the blond-haired boy at Jacob's side. "We've been waiting here for hours."

"Yeah, where's their reward?" I prodded.

"You'll get something, and you too, all of you, *Aiden especially.*" He grabbed me by the shirt and shoved me away.

"Where's Ethan?" I asked.

Jacob huffed.

"Thanks for the reminder. Hey Teddy! Bring him out!"

A pudgy kid with a bowl for a helmet went to the side of the house and came back with Ethan. I began to wonder just how many parents left their kids alone after school in this neighborhood. Other than Mr. Hanson, I hadn't even seen a car in a driveway.

"You okay, Ethan?" I asked.

"Yeah, Aiden, they flanked me good I guess," Ethan said.

"I'm sorry," I said.

"It's okay. We're still friends, right?" Ethan said.

"Of course." I smiled in relief, *one friend is more than none.*

"Good," Ethan smiled.

"That's enough," Jacob commanded.

"Gift card time," Orange said.

Jacob thought on it and then nodded. He reached into his pocket and pulled out a shiny red and black gift card. He tossed it to the ground and smiled as the hyenas leapt. The color brothers went for the card but slammed right into five of the front line kids who also dove at it.

A fistfight broke out in the pile of boys. Jacob

took immense pleasure in watching it go. I stood to the side, watching Jacob.

How could he enjoy such things? What made him this way?

"I got it!" Orange yelled as he raised the gift card high. The other kids scrambled up his leg, but the rest of the colors pushed them off and formed a circle.

"Pleasure doing business with you," Orange said as he got back on his bike.

"And the grades?" Red added.

"I hear you got straight A's this semester," Jacob said.

Red smiled.

The bike gang released their kickstands and took off up the hill and back to their cornfields. Some of the other kids went to leave too but Jacob stopped them with a glare.

"Looks like it's just you and me, Aiden," Jacob said with a joker's smile.

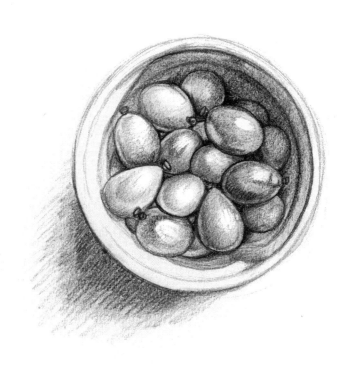

Jump

I took a moment to think. Although to most people, my thinking usually just looks like staring. I didn't know what I was doing, I still really don't know. I just know that at that moment, I had never been more afraid in my life. *Why must I always do things that scare me?*

"They're not your friends, Jacob," I said quietly.

"What was that?" Jacob asked as he drew his ear close to my mouth.

"They're not your friends," I whispered.

"Really?" Jacob laughed. "Hey guys, he says you aren't my friends." He forced a laugh and motioned the others to join him.

They did but they didn't want to, the same way people clap at a school play.

Jacob's face turned cold. "See? I'm the most popular kid in school," he said.

"They're just afraid of you," I said. "That doesn't make you popular."

"With good reason," he smiled.

"If they were your friends, you wouldn't have to bribe them," I said. "They would have just helped you get me without your needing to give them anything. Then again, what kind of friends would help bully someone?"

The other kids shifted uncomfortably, looking everywhere but at me and Jacob.

"What are we getting out of this, anyways?" asked Teddy, the chubby kid.

"Yeah, where's our gift card?" asked Michael, the blonde kid, again.

"He doesn't have anything for you," I yelled.

"Shut up!" Jacob shouted and slapped me with the back of his gun.

I winced and stared back at Jacob.

"You're a coward, Jacob," I said.

Jacob let out a fake laugh. "Hardy, har harr, Aiden. I'm not the one that's been running all day. You knew where to find me, where I'd be waiting for you, but instead you went for a little run with your friends. And where did that get you? One of them's tied up with me and the other? What's his name again?"

"Ben," I said.

"Oh yeah, the one you saved. Where is he?" Jacob taunted.

I said nothing.

"That's what I thought," Jacob grabbed me and untucked my shirt. "Melvin!"

Melvin came out from behind one of the barricades, carrying a bucket filled with waterballoons. Melvin always hung out with Jacob, though I don't think it was voluntary. Melvin did the things Jacob didn't want to do. The thing is he always looked like he was apologizing when he did them.

"Hello Aiden," Melvin said.

"Hey Melvin," I said back.

"Enough chit-chat," Jacob said as he shoved Melvin.

Melvin took out a waterballoon and stuffed it in my underwear.

"You could have done things the easy ways." Jacob said as Melvin stuffed another balloon down my pants. "Who knows, maybe I would have gone easy on you."

"Is that enough?" Melvin asked. "I don't think there's anymore room."

Jacob shoved Melvin aside and grabbed a balloon.

"There's more room," he said as he jammed another one in. "Look, there's tons more room. I could do this all day."

Melvin stepped back and looked at me. I nodded my head, as if to forgive him.

Jacob pulled out another balloon and stuffed it in my front pocket. "But you don't do things the easy way, do you? You just had to rat on me to my mom. She believed you, too. You know how long I'm grounded for? How much of summer I'm going to miss because of you?" Jacob put more balloons in my back pockets. "You could have done this easy, but no, you ran. You ran, and you know what that makes you?"

He pushed me backwards and I felt all of the water in the many balloons slap against my thighs. It felt cold, like I had wet myself.

I looked at him in the eyes.

"Say it, Aiden," Jacob commanded.

I refused.

"Say it," Jacob said as he stuffed a balloon down my shirt.

"Come on, Jacob, this isn't cool," Ethan said.

The other kids agreed, but they were too afraid to say anything.

"Am I talking to you?" Jacob snapped.

Ethan lowered his head and backed away.

I glared at Jacob. "You know what?" I said. "One day, the other kids are going to figure you out. They're going to be stronger, and smarter, and braver than you, and when that happens, you won't be able to control them anymore. And you'll be alone, Jacob, just like you fear."

Jacob scowled at me.

I held my ground.

"Jump," he said.

I refused.

"Is this worth it?" I asked the other kids. "Is a gift card and some water balloons all it takes to control us? He isn't going to stop. If you let him do this to me, you let him do it to all of us. What's to stop him from taking more?"

"I said jump!" Jacob screamed. He punched the balloon in my chest. It exploded. Cold water washed down my legs.

Some of the kids snickered.

"You want to spend the rest of grade school like this? What happens in Junior High?" I yelled.

The other kids stared at one another.

Jacob punched me again, popping the balloon in my front pocket. Water ran down my legs.

The crowd started to murmur.

"He only has power because we're afraid of him. Don't be afraid. Don't let him control you," I said.

Jacob kneed me in the stomach and popped two more balloons. Water splashed on the ground as I doubled over in pain.

"I SAID JUMP," Jacob snarled. He grabbed the rest of the water balloons out of the bucket and stuffed them down my shirt.

I stumbled back and felt the bruises forming on my skin.

Finally, I jumped.

One jumping jack. A balloon popped. Water flooded down my spine.

Jacob smiled.

Two jumping jacks. Another balloon popped. Water went down my chest. The other kids stared like beaten dogs.

Three jumping jacks. Two more balloons popped. Water went down my legs.

Ethan turned away.

Four jumping jacks.

"Stop," said one of the kids.

Five jumping jacks. More water hit the pavement.

"That's enough," said another boy.

Six jumping jacks.

"Stop!" someone called out.

I stopped.

Jacob turned around.

"Who said that?" he asked.

A redheaded boy stepped forward.

"I did," he said.

"Rusty Collins, step right up and join the other coward," Jacob said.

Jacob grabbed Rusty and started stuffing water balloons in his clothes. He refilled my pockets just for good measure. Rusty and I stayed still.

"Now jump," Jacob said.

Respite

"Car!" yelled Melvin.

"Retreat!" Jacob yelled.

The other kids grabbed their weapons and headed up the hill, away from my house. Jacob stayed behind to handle the adult.

I knew the van well; it belonged to Mom.

"Aiden?" She rolled down the window. "What are you boys doing out here?"

"Just playing pretend," Jacob said.

I wanted to say something. Rat out Jacob; call the police even. The kid belonged in a therapist's office, a mental institution, a jail, something. I looked over at Rusty's face though, and saw the eyes of a kid who was just barely hanging on.

That's when I realized something: this wasn't about me.

If I spoke up at that moment, if I turned Jacob in, then I would be sending the signal that the only way to stop Jacob is if an adult stepped in. They would fix it, sure, and it was always good to tell them what was going on, but Jacob already behaved when adults were around, so what would change when we were alone with him again?

"Sweetie, are you alright?" asked my mom. She looked tired from a long day of work. Some days she would come home early to make dinner, others we would all go out to eat. I guess today was my lucky day.

"Yeah, mom, I'm fine. We're just playing war, that's all. Are we having asparagus tonight? Asparagus is my favorite," I said.

I hate asparagus. My mom knew that too and got the message.

"Oh . . . Good to see you making friends," she said, "but can you ask them to move? They're blocking the garage."

"Let the nice lady through!" Jacob yelled to his stooges. They dragged aside the last of the barricades and made way for the van.

"Thanks. This heat though, right? You boys staying hydrated?" my mom asked.

"Yes, ma'am," Jacob said.

"We have plenty of water," I added, water still dripping down my legs.

She noticed that I was soaked but didn't say anything.

"Don't stay out too late," mom said.

"I won't."

My mom headed in with the groceries. Jacob made sure to wave to her as the door closed. He then turned his attention back to me.

"Finally showing a little bravery," Jacob said. "Now, where were we?"

"Sweetie!" mom yelled from the front porch.

Jacob snapped back into good boy mode.

"Yeah, mom?" I said.

"Did you forget something?" She asked.

I thought for a moment. This day had been too much; I couldn't even form a clue.

"No, what?" I said.

"You were supposed to do the dishes before I got home."

"Oh, yeah, sure," I said.

Jacob glared at me.

"Let me just finish up and I'll be right inside," I said.

"Okay," said my mom as she closed the front door.

"Your luck is trying my patience, Aiden," Jacob said.

"Sundown," I said.

"Sundown, what?" Jacob asked.

"We meet at the Dry Pond. No armies, no bounties. Just you, me, and a pair of water pistols," I said. "First one to get drenched loses."

"And what's in it for me?" Jacob asked.

"First day of school, I'll go wearing only my underwear."

Jacob snorted. "First week, maybe. And then after that you replace Melvin."

I looked over at Melvin who looked both happy and terrified for my safety.

"I'm not going to be your slave, Jacob," I said.

"Then we settle this now," he said, arms crossed.

"You don't have to fight him, Aiden," Ethan said. "Just tell your mom what's going on. Everything will work out. Jacob's reasonable."

"Listen to your dumb friend," Jacob said.

"Don't call him that," I commanded.

Jacob put his hands up, "I've seen his test scores. Don't get mad at me for calling a duck a duck."

I growled so hard my shirt vibrated.

"If I win, you leave us alone," I said as I gestured towards all of the other kids. "All of us."

"Deal. We settle this one on one. Then everyone is going to see just how much of a coward you are when you don't even show up," Jacob said. "I'm also keeping the duck as collateral."

Ethan stood by the side, too afraid to act. His face had fallen to a frown after being called dumb.

"You okay with staying with him?" I asked Ethan.

"If it helps you," Ethan said.

"You're not dumb," I said.

"Thank you, Aiden," Ethan said.

I looked back at Jacob.

"Deal," I said.

Jacob crossed his arms.

"I'll enjoy bossing you around," he said.

Preparations

I went inside and got to work on the dishes. Mom had already put away the groceries and it was only a matter of time before my father got home.

My mother stirred some mac n' cheese on the stove.

Mac n' cheese is my favorite food.

"Who's your new friend?" she asked.

I turned on the water and soaped up a sponge.

"Jacob," I said, trying not to put any inflection to the words.

"He seems nice," she lied.

"Seems is a good way to put it," I said as I dried the first plate.

"I didn't see Ben out there," she said. "You guys okay?"

I hate it when she pries, but honestly, I wish she had asked more questions. I wish I wouldn't have to tell her anything. That's the weird thing about talking to adults. You want them to know everything, but you don't want to have to say it; and the funny thing is, once you tell them what you don't want them to hear, they already knew it anyway! So why do they even ask?

"I don't know if we're friends anymore," I said softly.

"Oh? What happened?" she said as she cut the fire and strained the elbow noodles.

"I don't know," I lied. "We didn't really see things the same way."

Mom cut open the white cheese packet and tossed it into the pan with the noodles. I love that packet. It's so weird the way the orange globs stick together and somehow turn into cheese. If it's really cheese at all. It just tastes so good. I love it.

"Maybe you should give him a call after dinner," she suggested as she pulled out a packet of hot dogs and threw two franks in the microwave.

"I have to take care of something before it gets dark," I said.

"Oh?" she said as she leaned against the counter.

I looked at her feeling more like an equal than her son.

"Yeah," I said. "But I shouldn't be too late."

She nodded.

The microwave dinged. Mom pulled out the wieners and sliced them, adding them to the macaroni.

"Something to do with Jacob?" she asked, already knowing the answer.

"Yeah," I said.

"I figured." She added a touch of ketchup and threw the whole pot in a bowl. "Dad won't be home until later. Mr. Cardigan asked him to stay longer to get some of the Christmas shipments out."

"Christmas shipments?" I asked. "It's summer."

"Yeah, sweetie, Christmas ships in the summer and summer ships in winter, it's how things arrive on time," she said.

"Oh, I guess that makes sense," I said.

"Come sit, dinner's ready," she said.

I dried off the last dish and sat at the counter.

She slid the Mac N' Cheese over to me.

"Where's yours?" I asked.

"I'll eat later," she said.

I looked at her in the eyes. She wasn't telling me something.

"You know I have to go out there and meet Jacob, don't you?" I asked.

"That's why I made your favorite meal," she said.

"Thank you," I said with a slight smile.

She kissed me on the forehead and tussled my hair.

"Promise me something," she asked.

"Okay," I said, still staring at the dark orange noodles.

"Whatever you do, don't use violence, all right?" Her voice sounded serious.

I didn't have anything to say. I never wanted to hurt anyone, but then again I had to stand up to Jacob. I didn't have a choice. So if it came down to hitting him, I guess I had to.

"You're too smart to use your fists, Aiden," she said. "That's not the boy I love."

"How then?" I asked.

"You're a smart boy. You'll figure it out. Just promise me."

I nodded. "Yes, Mom."

"Promise."

"I promise, Mom."

"Good." She stood up. "I'm going to dinner with your father after he gets off work. You sure you can handle your friends?"

"Yeah," I said.

"Are you sure you're sure? I could call his mom if you want," she asked.

"Maybe if this doesn't work," I said.

"Be home by eight. Maybe if this has a happy ending I'll get you a gift card to GameStop." My mom smiled and kissed me on the forehead. "And if it doesn't, Mama bear will have to show some claws."

She headed to her bedroom to get ready for the night.

"How do you know about the gift card?" I asked, but she didn't say anything back. *How did she know? Did all of the parents know? How deep did this go?*

I put down my fork and grabbed the home phone.

It rang for a long minute.

No answer.

I checked the phone book and found another number, dialed, and waited another long minute.

"Hello?" came a voice that didn't want to be on the phone.

"Ben, it's me," I said.

He didn't say anything but I could hear the fabric of his shirt shifting around.

"Don't hang up," I pleaded.

"What do you want?" he finally said.

"You didn't pick up your cell phone," I said.

"Duh," he snapped back and I suddenly remembered how it had been drenched.

"I'll pay for it," I said.

"Maybe Jacob could afford a new one," Ben said. "He might be looking for a new friend."

"Don't say that," I said.

"Why did you call, Aiden? And make it quick, my mom is staring at me."

"I need your help."

"Oh, is that all? Did Ethan ever get home?" he asked.

"Not exactly," I said, not wanting to explain the situation.

"Oh, but you did though?" he came back.

"He's being held as collateral," I blurted.

"What did you do now?"

I didn't have the words.

"Ben, please, I think you owe me one," I said, though it was way more of a question.

"You'll help me pay for a new phone?" he asked.

"I don't know how, but yes, I will help you get a new phone," I promised.

"Then we're even?" Ben said.

I was so angry I could barely hold it in. How dare Ben say that to me, I was the one that stood up for him? After all, he was the reason I was in this mess in the first place!

"You know what, Ben? Maybe next time I'll let Jacob do whatever he wants to you. Maybe next time I'll just stand off to the side and watch, would you like that better?" I yelled. "I thought we were friends. I thought you had my back. That's why I stood up for you back there, because I thought you'd do the same for me!"

Silence.

"I'm sick of this. I'm sick of everyone being afraid just because his mom is the principal and his dad has money. It's not right. But you know what makes me different from the rest of you? I actually want to do something about it. I'm going down to the pond at sunset, and I'm going to stand up to him."

"Stand up for what?" Ben asked.

"Everyone, Ben, everyone he's hurt, the kids who are afraid of him, you, me, *the cowards*, Ben."

Ben still didn't say anything. I didn't know whether that meant I moved him with my words or that I was screaming at a brick wall.

"Let me think," he said quickly and then hung up.

I put the phone back in its cradle, sat down, and let my head drop over my food.

I pulled my hair so hard that some of it fell into my mac n' wieners.

Gross.

I pushed the food away and thought.

Think, Aiden, think. What can we do?

I grabbed the bowl and headed for the trash can to waste the cheesy goodness.

I stopped.

I looked at the big black trash bag lining the bin. It had a familiar look to it, slick, stretchy, like something I had seen before.

"Huh," I said to myself.

Alone

"You need anything before we go, sweetie?" my mom asked from the hall.

"I'm fine," I called back. I took the red band of a trash bag and yanked it tight, turned off the faucet, and slung a towel over my shoulder.

"Bye then, love you!" she called.

"Love you, too," I said. I hit the garage door opener for my parents and watched as they pulled out of the driveway. My mom waved back and blew me a kiss. It felt good to have someone believe in me.

I looked over my supplies and the little red wagon straining to hold it all. Just one thing left to do. I picked the phone back up, checked the number list, and left a handful of messages.

A few minutes later, I shut the garage door and started the long walk downhill to the pond, dragging the little red wagon behind me.

Careful, I thought. *No sudden movements. Nice and easy does it.*

Downfall

When the neighborhood was first developed, way before we moved here, one of the main features was a man-made pond about the size of two football fields. The pond fed most of the creeks and smaller ponds that dotted the neighborhood.

The pond has a huge overflow drain in the southwest corner that's there to prevent flooding. Since the drought started though, the pipe hasn't been necessary and now it stands there, a big concrete cylinder jutting ten feet out of the ground, a monument to the drought.

To me, it looked like a tombstone.

Behind me, I dragged a small red wagon, the kind that many an afternoon of my younger years had been spent playing with. Inside there was a wiggling black bag, my backup plan.

An army waited for me at the Dry Pond. My feet kicked up dirt from the parched, cracked ground as I walked. The sun had set far to the west, our light came from a pale moon, and a handful of dim orange street lights.

Jacob stood in the center, gold-painted water pistols in both hands. I glared at him from under my brow.

Behind him stood a row of the meanest kids in school, or should I say the weakest, hard to tell the difference. Each one of them had their own Super Soaker.

Beyond the shock troop were the rest of Jacob's goons. Who knew what he said to get them there? How many gift cards had he promised? Or were they just afraid of him like everyone else? Melvin led the pack. He had a cell phone in hand ready to dial, probably to call Jacob's mom if he started to lose.

"I got to be honest," Jacob said, "I didn't think you'd show."

"Are you not honest very often?" I said.

He laughed.

"Where's Ethan?" I asked.

"Hey Frank, bring him out," Jacob said.

A kid about twice Jacob's height stood up and dragged Ethan into the center of the dry pond bed. Frank Maloney was big, too big. He had grown quicker than all the rest of the kids in Junior High. *Wait-* Jacob brought junior high kids into this? How many others were there?

I looked over the crowd and saw all of the heads that stood higher than the rest. While I had been having comfort food, Jacob had been making calls. He watched me count and grinned.

"I guess I had you pegged wrong, Aiden. I half expected you not to show," Jacob said.

"Then why did you bring junior high kids into this?" I asked.

"I said half expected," Jacob sneered. "You gotta be prepared if you want to rule this neighborhood."

"Are you okay?" I asked Ethan as he was forced next to Jacob.

"I don't want to play this anymore," Ethan said. While I had been eating my last meal, Jacob had been subjecting Ethan to every form of water abuse that he couldn't do to me. The poor kid looked like he had just gotten out of a desert rainstorm.

"It will be over soon," I said as I coaxed him behind me.

"Grab him," Jacob ordered. Frank and another kid his size stepped through the line and grabbed me by the shoulders. They dragged me to Jacob and threw me down on my knees.

"I thought this was a duel," I said as I tried to get up. Frank put his foot on my back and forced me to kneel. Jacob strutted to my back.

"I like this better," Jacob said. He pushed Frank aside and put his shoe on my spine. It looked like one of those images you see in history books: the dictator stepping on the back of a commoner, one foot on the shoulder, the other one under the commoner's face.

I felt like a shoe shine box.

"All you have to do is kiss my shoe, Aiden. Kiss it and this will all be over."

The thought crossed my mind. He had his other foot right under my head; all it would take was a little bend.

"Kiss it!" Jacob yelled, as he pressed down harder.

I pushed his foot off me, but the sixth graders shoved me back down.

The other kids watched. I saw pain in their eyes. They wanted to do something but they couldn't. To them, Jacob was a fact of life. He had always been with them, and as far as they could see, he would always be there. Me though, I was new. I had only suffered Jacob for eight months. That made me special. I could do something they couldn't.

"Is this worth it?" I yelled at the kids.

Jacob stepped down again. "You're alone, Aiden."

"How long are you going to let him do this?" I yelled to the kids again.

"They're not listening," he growled.

"Is this the school that you want? Is this the neighborhood you want?" I shouted.

"Kiss —my —shoe," Jacob ordered.

"Stand up to him!" I yelled.

"Kiss it," Jacob said, lording over me.

His shoe was so close to my face I could smell the new shoe smell. Expensive shoes, the kind any kid would want for a birthday but Jacob's was back in January.

Jacob smiled.

Then it hit him —a blast right in the chest from a huge water gun.

Jacob fell back, caught in the arms of the sixth graders.

"Get off him," Ben stepped behind me.

I didn't want to stand up. I was scared, and I didn't want to keep going.

I stood anyway.

"Join me," I said looking out at the other kids, "and this can end tonight."

Dirt bikes roared in the distance. We all watched as the cavalry rode in. Dust settled on the pond, and the four colors took off their bike helmets.

"Join me," I said, "And we can end this."

One kid crossed the line and stood behind me, then another kid came, and then two more. Jacob gritted his teeth.

Three more crossed.

"Cowards!" he yelled, but half his army now stood behind me. "I'll make sure every last one of you rots in summer school!"

"You see that? He's scared," I said. "He can't change everyone's grades, his mom would find out."

Two more kids joined my side.

Jacob only had sixth graders left. I turned to them.

"What's he paying you?" I asked. "What's he threatening you with?"

"More than you got," Jacob said, "Go ahead, guys, join him. See if I care. You'll pay, all of you."

"What happened to you, Jacob? Don't you want friends? Don't you want people to like you?" I asked. "When did it go wrong? When did you start lashing out and hurting people to make yourself feel better?"

"Shut up!" Jacob yelled as he pulled out his water guns and pointed them at me. His hands were trembling; something must have gotten to him.

"We could hang out. You could come to my house. We could watch a movie. We could go to Six Flags," I said with my arms raised. "You don't have to be alone, man. Nobody deserves to be alone."

"I'd never hang out with a dork like you. You're the lowest rung on the school ladder. An outcast. No one cares about you. You've had a whole year here, and look at how many friends you have. Two. Two friends, and you want to preach to me?"

I shook my head.

"I have two more friends than you do, Jacob," I said.

Jacob fired.

The other kids followed. The sixth graders raised their Super Soakers and started blasting.

Water sprayed across the dirt. Kids shrieked as the cold water hit their skin. They fell to the ground in a pool of ever –expanding mud.

Ben grabbed me and pulled me out of the fray.

Streams crisscrossed the air. Kids screamed. Water splattered. It felt like a water park had been turned upside down and all the water from all the rides had come crashing down. I've seen thunderstorms with less water.

"My phone!" yelled one of them. A gush of water hit his face.

All around me kids were getting soaked. They pumped their guns and sprayed wildly into the air. There must have been gallons of friendly fire. The ground took most of the pain though, and soon we were all stumbling through gooey mud.

A group of four surrounded a sixth grader and hosed him from all sides. He screamed and fell.

"It's so cold!" he shrieked.

Another sixth grader pushed forward, carving a path through kids with a single shot. He pumped the gun, readying another blast, and took aim at Ethan.

Ben sniped a shot right into the sixth grader's eye. The kid squealed, grabbed his eyes, and dropped his Super Soaker.

"No fair, you little punk!" shouted the sixth grader.

I reached down, grabbed his gun, and joined Ben in a retreat.

"Fall back to the wagon!" I called out.

Soaked soldiers fell all around me. Many a cell phone was ruined; many a shirt stained; many a pride would never be the same.

"What's the plan?" Ben yelled. A blast of water shot past his shoulder. He cocked his gun, swiveled back, and returned fire.

"Ice water!" shrieked the kid.

"More where that came from!" shouted Ben.

We reached the wagon and I pulled out a backpack. Some of the kids who had sided with me ran up and joined us.

"Towels!" I yelled as I tossed them out.

Ben and the others tucked them into the tops of their shirts and slung the other end over their arms. It formed a shield that they could deflect, or at least absorb, a good hit with.

"Lock arms and push forward," Ben shouted. The kids looked at each other, nodded, and did as they were told. Together they marched into the pond towards a formation of sixth graders. It looked like something out of a classic Greco-Roman strategy –a single group of kids wrapped together like a turtle surrounded on all sides by enemies twice their size. They held strong and, when the time was right, fired as if they were one kid and took out each sixth grader.

"Fall back!" screamed the largest of the sixth graders. The other ran with him but my friends gave chase.

"Yes!" I shouted as I jumped for joy. That's when a water balloon hit my face.

I looked over and saw Jacob.

He shoved through the crowd and shrugged off a shot from the rear of the formation. He turned around and clapped two water balloons together, sending a horizontal waterfall right at the kid. It hit and the back of the formation fell.

"Aiden!" he screamed as he threw another balloon.

I ducked behind a towel. The balloon exploded and threw water to the sides. I wrapped up the towel and whipped it at him. He caught the other end and yanked it right out of my hands, flinging it to the ground and squashing it into the mud.

"That was my grandma's" I cursed.

"Then you should have left it at home!" Jacob cried as he tackled me. I caught him and we flew to the mud, rolling in it until our clothes were caked in brown.

"I'm glad you didn't do this the easy way," Jacob said, as he pulled out his golden guns and pointed them at my face.

"You really know how to make a mess of things, Jacob," I said, as I tried to push the guns away from my face.

Jacob pulled the triggers but the shot flew wide as another fierce stream slammed into his face. He tumbled to the ground then stood up, holding a fresh red mark on his face.

"Get away from him, cootie walrus," said Veronica as she lowered the Eaudezeus.

Jimmy helped me up.

"You okay?" he asked.

"Yeah, thanks. What, why?" I stumbled.

Jimmy shrugged. "He's a terrible client," he said.

"And a big meanie," said Jimmy's sister.

"You're both dead to me," Jacob said, as he wiped the water from his hair. "The bathrooms, the lockers, don't expect to get any business done in there next year."

"Doesn't look like you'll be in control much longer, friend," Jimmy said as he held the gun back up.

"Just back off, Jacob. You're out-gunned and outnumbered, you've lost. Give it up," I said.

Jacob laughed. "When I'm done with you, you're gonna have to transfer," he growled.

Jacob ran at Jimmy's sister. She fired and an intense stream of water splattered right into his chest. Jacob howled with pain but charged through it, grabbed the gun, and turned it on her. Within a few seconds, she was drenched and screaming for her mommy.

Jimmy pulled out his gun and shot at Jacob, but the bully was in a frenzy and took the hits like they were air. He grabbed Jimmy by the wrist, twisted it back, and made him fire water right in his face.

"Stop soaking yourself," Jacob cackled.

"Jimmy!" cried his sister as she ran for the street. Jimmy looked at Jacob.

"This isn't over," he said and he took off after her.

I retreated to the wagon and the very large, quivering black bag.

"Where you going, Aiden? Aren't we having fun?" Jacob taunted.

"Stay back, Jacob. I'm warning you," I said, as I hunched next to the wagon.

Jacob ran for me but a spray hit his face. He turned and saw Ben who, up until just then, had been fighting with the other kids.

"You," Jacob said.

"What's it to you?" Ben said.

Jacob pulled out a small gun from his back waistband and fired a quick shot at Ben. It connected with his face and my friend screamed in pain.

"Lemon juice!" Ben howled. He rubbed his eyes and fell back.

"Ben!" I yelled and scrambled for him. Jacob ran up to me and shoved me to the ground. I rolled and found myself on my back, Jacob over me.

"How about this?" he said, as he laughed. He put the small gun to my eyes and fired. A squirt of lemon went straight into my eyes. It felt like a hundred hornets stinging.

I opened my red eyes, and saw his smiling face through the blurriness.

"What are you?" I whispered, as I pulled myself toward the wagon.

"Your worst nightmare," he answered.

I didn't know what to do. My eyes hurt. My body hurt. I was covered in mud and my best friends had all been hurt. Every kid in the neighborhood was soaked or out of commission and it was all my fault. If I had never thrown that balloon, none of this would have happened. Why? Why did I stand up to this monster? What made me think I could take him? What made me think I could stop him?

"Oh, I know that look," Jacob said. "Hold still, I want a picture." Jacob reached into his pocket and pulled out his cell phone. It had been wrapped in a sandwich bag so that none of the water could touch it. "Pretty clever, right?"

Ben groaned and rolled on his side.

"It burns," he said. "You're a dirty cheat, Jacob."

"I'm a dirty, cheating, winner, and you better remember that," Jacob said.

Jacob fired a single shot and hit him square in the eyes.

Ben cried.

"You got something in your eyes," Jacob pulled the trigger lightly, and lemon juice stung my face.

I screamed.

Jacob took the phone out of the plastic bag and

snapped a selfie of himself and me with my bloodshot eyes.

"What makes you think I won't soak us both?" I said through tears.

"What? Your bag of water balloons? Not much use if they're still in the bag. Face it, chump, you've lost. I've won. Even if all the sixth graders run, I've still won. You're mine. From here until you graduate college, your every waking minute is going to be wet. I'm going to make sure of it."

"Jacob," I said slowly, "listen carefully. My parents won't let me have a phone."

I held up a butter knife I had smuggled from home and pointed it right at the quivering black bag. Jacob's eyes went wide with the realization: the black trash bag, the one the size of a small refrigerator that wiggled and bounced at the slightest touch, was not filled with water balloons, *it was a water balloon.*

I plunged the knife deep into the bag.

A gush of water shot out, slamming right into Jacob's face.

He screamed as his unprotected phone tumbled through the water and landed in the mud.

The wave of water rushed down to the center of

the pond and washed the fight right out of the crowd.

Jacob ran to the phone, water dripping from every pore on his skin, and picked it up like a terrified kitten. He wiped it clean, tried to dry it with his wet clothes, and held it close to his chest. I'd never seen him so scared.

Just like Ben, he tried to turn on his phone again and again, but the phone wouldn't respond, and the more he tried the more desperate he became.

The other kids recovered from the water fight and gathered around to see why Jacob was crying. They were all covered in mud, shell-shocked, and tired, but the spectacle of the biggest bully in school freaking out couldn't be missed.

"Why you little —I ought to —I should," he shouted as he hit the unlock button repeatedly.

"What's wrong, Jacob?" I asked softly.

"You're gonna —I swear, you, you're gonna pay for a new one."

Jacob dropped to his knees and curled up in a ball.

He cried.

The other kids encircled him. They'd never seen a bully cry before.

Ben gave me a hand up. I stood and joined the circle.

Jacob stammered more threats through tears. He spoke of what would happen to all of us if we didn't stop watching. How much we would suffer, how horrible the next school year would be. Yet, no one left. We all just watched him cry. It was like watching a sponge dry out. All that mass, that bluster, was nothing but show, and when he fell apart, we got to see what he was really made of.

Jacob was a coward.

We won, true, but none of us expected that we'd feel *sorry* for Jacob. Pull back the tough talk, the threats, the abuse, and what do you have? A scared little kid, that's all. Just like the rest of us.

"Let's go home," I said.

We left Jacob in the muddy pond bed, curled up like a baby, crying, the mud drying around him.

That night, for the first time in six months, it rained.

The drought had ended.

Reparations

Ethan cradled a bowl of ice cream on my couch as Ben navigated the last level of a new video game. I sat on the bar stool near the kitchen, watching over them, thinking.

It had been five days since the last day of school, and I still didn't know what to think of it. Had I made a difference? What would next year bring? When were Jacob's parents going to call mine?

The doorbell rang.

Ben paused the game. Ethan put down his spoon. I stood and headed for the door.

Jacob stood there like a lost dog.

My heart sank to my stomach. Part of me was ready to fight, another part of me figured that he wouldn't be able to fight back.

Ben and Ethan looked at each other, waiting for me to make a call.

"Hi," Jacob said. He sounded like a mouse, unsure of a trap.

"Hello," I replied, trying not to sound like anything at all.

We stood there for a moment, not knowing what to say.

I looked past him and saw his mother sitting in the car with the window rolled down. He had been forced to come here.

Jacob looked at the floor for peace.

"It's okay," I said. "You don't have to say anything."

Jacob nodded.

"You're not a coward, Aiden," he said softly.

"Thank you," I said. "What about your phone?"

"Oh, that, yeah. Maybe for Christmas? I don't know. I'm kind of grounded until I'm thirty," Jacob said.

"There will be a better phone out by then," I said.

"Yeah. It's my fault," Jacob said. "I get that now."

I couldn't believe what I was hearing. Yet, there was Jacob Shull, the biggest bully in school, looking like a broken horse.

"Truce?" I said, offering a handshake.

"Truce," Jacob said and he shook my hand.

He turned to leave, his mother watching his every move. He got about halfway down the driveway when an odd thought popped into my mind. A thought that, much like so many of my other thoughts, I never should have acted on.

"Hey Jacob," I called.

He stopped and turned back. "Yeah?"

"My mom's taking us to the water park Saturday. You wanna come?" I said. I couldn't believe that I made the offer, but the kid seemed whipped. He looked just like me on the first day of school a year ago when everyone was new, and no one wanted to try and be friends. The kind of kid I looked like just eight short months ago.

Jacob closed his eyes like he was about to cry.

"No one's ever wanted to hang out with me," Jacob said.

"Is that a yes then?" I asked.

"I have to ask my mom," he said with a smile.

69358724R00075

Made in the USA
Middletown, DE
05 April 2018